THE CROCODILE AND THE DENTIST

BY TARO GOMI

F. Gomi

THE MILLBROOK PRESS
BROOKFIELD, CONNECTICUT

Library of Congress Cataloging-in-Publication Data
Gomi, Taro.
[Wani-san doki, haisha-san doki, Japanese]
The crocodile and the dentist / by Taro Gomi,
p.   cm.
Summary: A crocodile and a dentist have an
encounter in which each is afraid of the other.
ISBN 1-56294-555-6 (lib. ed.) ISBN 1-56294-845-8 (tr. ed.)
[1. Crocodiles—Fiction. 2. Dentists—Fiction.] I.Title.
PZ7.G568Cr   1994
[E]—dc20   94-20306   CIP   AC

The Crocodile and the Dentist by Taro Gomi
Copyright © 1984 by Taro Gomi
English text © 1994 by The Millbrook Press
Originally published in 1984 in Japanese
under the title *Wani-San Doki Haisha-San Doki*
by Kaisei-Sha Publishing Co., Ltd.
English translation rights arranged through
Japan Foreign-Rights Centre

First Published in the United States by
The Millbrook Press
2 Old New Milford Road
Brookfield, Ct 06804

I *really* don't want to see him. . .

but I must.

I *really* don't want to see him,
but I must.

Aaugh!

Shall I go through
with it. . . . ?

I must be brave.

I must be brave.

I'm ready for the worst.

I'm ready for the worst.

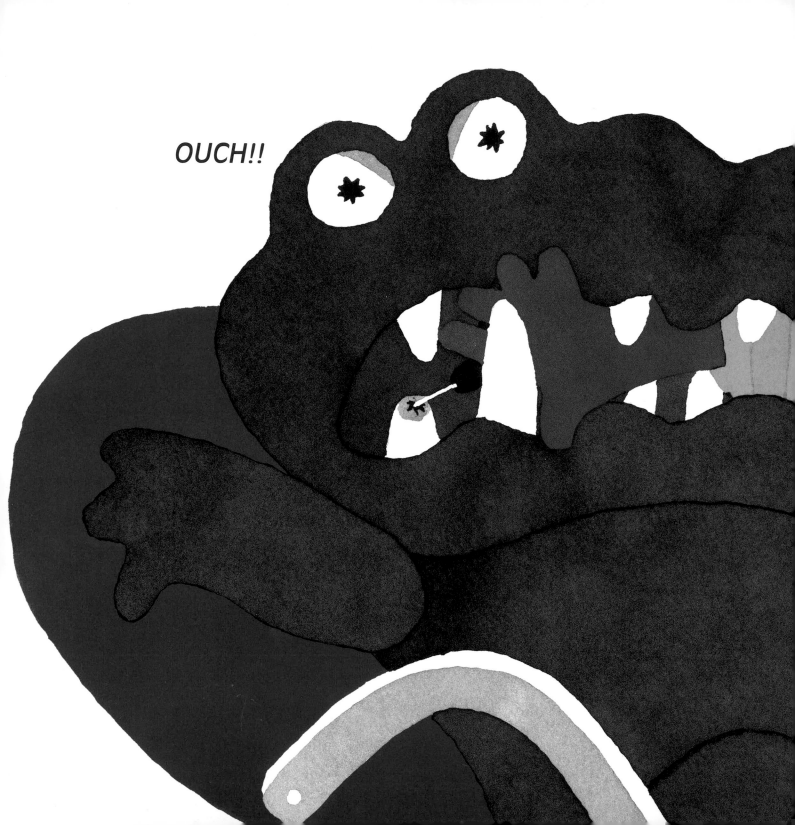

What an awful thing
to do.

What an awful thing
to do.

But getting angry
won't help.

But getting angry
won't help.

Not much longer. . .

Not much longer. . .

Whew. . .

Thank you so much.
See you again
next year.

Thank *you* so much.
See you again
next year.

I don't really want to see
him again next year. . .

I don't really want to see
him again next year...

So I must never
forget to brush my teeth.

G. TARO.

So you must never
forget to brush your teeth.